This is

THE CARNIVAL
with Mr. & Mrs. Bumba

When Mr. Bumba and Mrs. Moon become Mr. and Mrs. Bumba, exciting adventures are sure to follow.

Read all 10 books
— written by Pearl Augusta Harwood

You will also enjoy . . .

THE CARNIVAL

with Mr. and Mrs. Bumba

by
Pearl Augusta Harwood

pictures by
George Overlie

published by
Lerner Publications Company
Minneapolis, Minnesota

International Standard Book Number: 0-8225-0128-7
Library of Congress Catalog Card Number: 76-156360

Second Printing 1973

One day Bill and Jane and Nicky and Lee ran over to Mr. and Mrs. Bumba's house.

"Will they do it?" asked Niccolina, who was called Nicky for short.

"Of course they will," said Jane.

"They always help us when we ask them," said Bill.

"Mr. and Mrs. Bumba can do almost anything," said Lee.

Mrs. Bumba saw them coming. She was weeding in the garden.

"You all look as if you had something important to say," said Mrs. Bumba with a smile.

"Oh, we do," said Jane. "It's about the school carnival."

"We have one in May every year," said Bill.

"My mother would like you both to be on her committee," said Lee.

"What committee does she have?" asked Mrs. Bumba.

"The committee in charge of the whole carnival," said Lee.

Mr. Bumba came out of the kitchen door to listen.

"But we don't know anything about carnivals," he said.

"You know about building," said Bill. "The committee would like you to put up the booths for the carnival."

"Oh — I guess I could do that," said Mr. Bumba.

"And Mrs. Bumba knows how to sell things that people make, so the committee wants her to work in the gift booth," said Nicky.

"Oh — I guess I could do that," said Mrs. Bumba.

"Then I'll tell my mother that you both would like to be on her committee," said Lee.

"All right," said Mr. Bumba, smiling a wide smile. "We'll do the best we can to help."

The day of the carnival was two weeks away.

Mr. Bumba was in the Make-It Room building frames for the booths.

"What happened to the booths from last year?" he asked Bill and Lee.

"There weren't any," said Bill.

"And it rained, so everything on the tables got wet," said Lee. "It rained on all the cakes and pies and cookies and on all the things that people made."

"We'll put some canvas over the tops," said Mr. Bumba. "Then the booths will be protected from the rain and the sun."

Mrs. Bumba was weaving some little rugs on a loom. She was going to sell them at the carnival. There were two other looms in the Make-It Room. Jane and Nicky were weaving rugs too.

"Is the carnival just for fun?" asked Mrs. Bumba.

"It's for fun," said Jane. "But the money we make will buy books for our school library."

"Then we'll give them as many things to sell as we can," said Mrs. Bumba.

Lee came running over from his house.

"Oh, Mr. Bumba," he said. "My mother sent me over to ask you to help us out."

"What is the trouble?" asked Mr. Bumba.

"The teacher who leads our band is sick," said Lee, "so the band can't play at the carnival."

"That's too bad," said Mr. Bumba. "But what can I do about it?"

"You play a harmonica," said Lee. "You can teach us some harmonica songs. You can lead a harmonica band for the music program."

Mr. Bumba scratched his head. "How many boys and girls have harmonicas?" he asked.

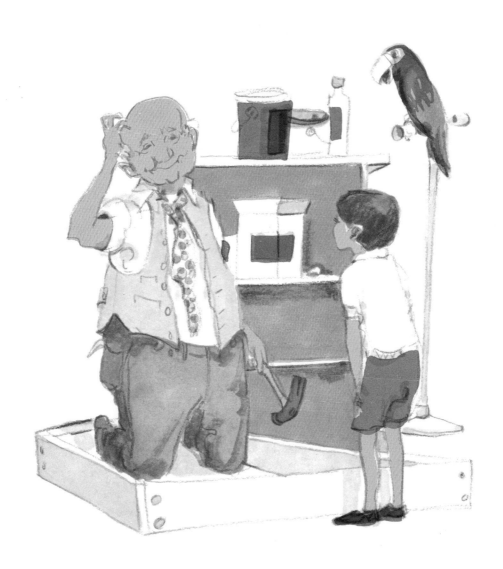

"Seven of us — all boys," said Lee. "Please help us. We MUST have music on the carnival program."

"All right," said Mr. Bumba, smiling a wide smile. "We'll practice every afternoon. I'll do what I can."

The next day Jane came running over from her house.

"Oh, Mrs. Bumba," she said. "My mother wants you to help us out."

"What is the trouble?" asked Mrs. Bumba.

"The woman who runs the gift booth at the carnival is sick," said Jane. "My mother would like you to take charge of it."

"Well, I suppose I can," said Mrs. Bumba. "If I can get enough people to help me."

"Oh, thank you!" said Jane. "My mother couldn't find anyone else to do it."

The next day Bill came running over from his house.

"Oh, Mr. and Mrs. Bumba," he said. "The two clowns have had to go away and can't be at the carnival. My mother would like you both to wear their costumes and be the clowns at the carnival. Will you?"

"Clowns!" said Mrs. Bumba.

"Clowns!" said Mr. Bumba.

"All you have to do is act funny and run around among the people," said Bill.

"But we don't know anything about how to act funny!" said Mr. Bumba.

"You just say funny things and do funny things," said Bill. "I'm sure you could do it."

"Well, we'll have to think about it," said Mrs. Bumba. "I'm afraid we don't know how to be clowns."

"I have an idea," said Mr. Bumba. "Why can't some boys or girls do it?"

"The costumes would be too large," said Lee, who had just come over.

"Why can't some of the teachers do it?" asked Mrs. Bumba.

"They are all busy with other things," said Lee.

"Why must you have clowns?" asked Mr. Bumba.

"We ALWAYS have two clowns at the carnival," said Bill. "People would be very disappointed not to see any."

"Well," said Mrs. Bumba. "Well . . . ."

"We could try," said Mr. Bumba with a very small smile.

On the day of the carnival Mr. and Mrs. Bumba went over to the schoolyard very early. Some of the fathers were there to help Mr. Bumba set up the booths.

Mrs. Bumba helped the mothers set up tables in the booths.

At twelve o'clock the carnival began. There was a big picnic in the schoolyard. All the children and their parents had as many hot dogs as they could eat, and ice cream for dessert.

After the picnic there was a program on the outdoor stage. The sixth grade gave a short play and the fourth grade gave one too. Then the room that Bill and Jane and Lee and Nicky were in did some folk dances. After that, Mr. Bumba's harmonica band played some songs. People clapped very hard for the band.

Then Lee and Bill ran up to Mr. Bumba. "It's time to put on your clown costumes!" said Bill. "We must hurry and find Mrs. Bumba."

Jane and Nicky found Mrs. Bumba at the gift booth. "They are looking for you and Mr. Bumba," said Jane. "Your clown costumes are all ready for you."

Mr. and Mrs. Bumba went to the dressing room behind the outdoor stage. They put the clown costumes on over their own clothes. Lee's mother helped them paint their faces in funny clown smiles.

"We still don't know how to act like clowns," said Mrs. Bumba. "But at least we'll LOOK like them."

Just then Lee's dog came running up to them. "Oh, Rex, go home!" said Lee's mother. "How did you get out of the yard!"

But Lee's dog wanted to play. He wanted to play with his friend Mr. Bumba. He took hold of Mr. Bumba's clown costume.

"Here, let that alone!" said Mr. Bumba, pulling away from him.

The dog pulled harder. The clown costume ripped all the way down the back. It was lucky that Mr. Bumba had on his own clothes underneath.

Mr. Bumba ran out toward the booths
with Lee's dog after him. The dog thought
it was a good game.

"A pin!" called Mr. Bumba. "I need a
pin, quick!"

Everyone who looked at him began to
laugh.

"What a funny, funny clown!" said one
little girl.

"He needs a whole bunch of pins!"
said a boy.

Mrs. Bumba was all dressed in her clown costume. She ran out after Mr. Bumba.

"Wait for me!" she called. "We'll have to find some pins somewhere! Here, Rexy, Rexy, come away, please!"

Mrs. Bumba kept trying to pull the dog away. The dog kept trying to pull Mr. Bumba's costume. Mr. Bumba kept asking people for pins. All the people who saw them laughed and laughed.

"That's the best clown act I ever saw!" said one of the fathers. "How do you train a dog to do that!"

At last Mr. and Mrs. Bumba saw that they didn't need to try to be funny because everyone thought they WERE funny. So they sat down on two chairs beside the ice cream booth and laughed and laughed at themselves. Lee's dog thought the game was over. He sat down, too, with his tongue hanging out.

Bill and Lee and Nicky and Jane came along to thank Mr. and Mrs. Bumba for being clowns.

"You can take off those costumes now," said Bill. "There's just one more little part to the program."

"Maybe we'd better go home now," said Mrs. Bumba, "if it's almost over."

"Oh, no, you mustn't go home yet!" Jane cried. "What's coming now may be the best part of all."

Mrs. Bumba got out of her costume and Mr. Bumba got out of what was left of his. They sat down with all the other people to see what the school principal was going to say.

"Every year at carnival time we give some awards," he began. He held up some squares of blue silk with gold letters on them.

There was an award for the "Mother of the Year."

There was an award for the "Father of the Year."

There was an award for the "Teacher of the Year."

Then the principal said, "This year we have one more award — one we never thought of before. This award is for 'Our Best Friends.'" He stopped a minute. Then he said, "I am happy to give this award to our REALLY best friends who ALWAYS help us out when we need them—Mr. and Mrs. A. C. Bumba!"

The hand clapping was very, very loud. But Lee and Jane and Nicky and Bill clapped loudest of all.